THE REINCARNATION OF RADHA

Mae Gosaynie

ISBN 978-93-5438-718-0

First published in India 2021 by Leadstart Inkstate
A Division of One Point Six Technologies Pvt Ltd

Sales Office:
119-123, 1st Floor, Building J2, B - Wing,
Wadala Truck Terminal, Wadala East,
Mumbai 400022, Maharashtra, INDIA
Phone: +91 96999 33000
Email: info@leadstartcorp.com
www.leadstartcorp.com

Disclaimer: The views expressed in this book are those of the Author and do not pertain to be held by the Publisher.

Editor: Sanjhee Gianchandani
Cover: R. Maharajan
Layouts: Kshitij Dhawale

To Lord Krishna,

You are my love, my life, the very breath of me, and you have command of every fiber of my being to live or die for thee.

About the Author

Mae Gosaynie is a citizen of the United States born to parents of Middle Eastern descent. She possesses two Bachelor's degrees: One in Biology and a second in English language and literature. She has a Master's degree or M.Ed. in Curriculum and Instruction with an emphasis on Differentiated Instruction. She also has a certified professional license to teach grades 6-12 and teaches Advanced Placement Biology and Human Anatomy at a High School in her home state of Michigan. She is a published author of an article entitled, "Acknowledging the Creator Within", published in Nature of Occurrences (Thought Notebook Journal) Thought Collection Publishing (TCP), Journal Issue 3 printed December 2, 2014. Found at the following link: https://www.amazon.com/Nature-Occurrences-Thought-Notebook-Journal/dp/099666355X

Mae's parents belonged to a religious sect that believed in reincarnation and the suffering of the soul, so these religious and spiritual concepts were ingrained in her upbringing early on. She chose to be born to this Middle eastern family in the U.S. so that she could learn about discrimination and racial inequality.

Her education was disrupted multiple times as she was transferred from one school to another. However, all these disruptions had a purpose. They exposed her to different racial demographics as well as different religious beliefs. By the time she was an adult woman she had taken communion in a Catholic church, prayed on her knees to Allah in a Muslim mosque, chanted Wahe Guru in a Sikh temple, and also experienced the Unified Field of Consciousness through her many years of practicing Transcendental Meditation. She was initiated into the TM movement in the fall of 1994. She progressed to advanced Siddha status and Yogi flying in 2003.

Mae has three sons from a previous marriage. She lives in a humble home with her small dog and youngest son. She lives her life in an attempt to help and guide others. She spends her days writing poetry, reading, taking long nature walks, and reciting 'Hare Krishna'.

About the Illustrator

Dalia Najjar is an uprising eighteen-year-old artist from Baakline, Lebanon. She inherited her artistic talents from both her parents who are Fine Arts majors and inspirational art teachers in the region. They mentored her and helped her artistic talents to flourish. Dalia has participated in and displayed drawings in many collective, national, and international exhibitions in her home country. The international ones that deserve mentioning are those organized through The United Nations and The World Wildlife Organization. She has been awarded recognition and prizes such as "The Sustainable Development Goals from Contemporary Art's Perspective" in 2019 organized by the United Nations and more recently the "2020 World Wildlife Day Global Youth Art Contest in collaboration with IFAW".

Her artwork is well-known to exemplify the two genres "micro art" and " zen tangle art" which means objects drawn in great detail with black ink and colored pencils.

Dalia's future plans are to attend college and to major in Architecture (the art we live in) so that she can perceive art from its many different perspectives.

Artwork page:
* Instagram: @dalia_diva
Contact:
* Email: dalianajjar222@gmail.com

Contents

I
Radha Creates Her Destiny

You are the creator of your destiny! However, that does not imply the choices you make here on Earth. Being the creator of your destiny refers to the choices you made prior to being born on this Earth. You chose to be born a male, a female, or a transgender. You chose your race and nationality. You chose the family you would be born to. You chose the time and location of your birth. All these choices were made to provide you with the life lessons your consciousness needed to evolve. Only in your final lifetime once the consciousness has become spiritually awakened by a Guru, a TM teacher, a Yoga teacher, or even through religious and loving pursuits, will you realize your potential to be a God. The same was true for Radha.

Radha knew this was going to be her final lifetime before she was born. However, Radha was a soul who did not love herself. Her lack of self-love could more accurately be described as self-loathing. She felt deeply that she would only deserve the blessing of enlightenment after a life saturated with a plethora of emotionally and physically painful experiences. So, she planned to be born into a Middle Eastern family that had emigrated to the U.S so she would be discriminated against. She planned to be born a middle sibling to suffer the unfairness of having to always wear hand-me-down clothes and to have her younger brother favored for being the heir to the family name. She had chosen to be raised an orphan and have her father, and dearest ally, die early in her life. She had chosen to be married to a man who was both controlling and emotionally and physically abusive. She had chosen her in-laws to be controlling so that they dictated what she wore and whom she visited. She had chosen to bear three sons who were highly educated, of good moral fiber, and kind. And those three sons, the blessing she had gifted to herself had chosen Radha, The Divine Mother, to carry them in her womb and to be suckled at her breast.

Radha also knew that during this lifetime, she would meet her soulmate, Lord Krishna. Women for centuries have talked and dreamt of their wish to meet their soulmates or twin flames, as it is referred to in astrological terms. What they do not comprehend is that such a meeting only happens in your final lifetime on this Earth. Only after you have lived many lives and experienced what it is to be a pauper, a wealthy aristocrat, a scholar, a man, a woman, an abuser, a victim, etc. will that soul be ready to meet its twin. He will be the Yang to your Yin. Or if you are a man, then she will be the Yin to your Yang. The same was true for Radha-Krishna. The only problem was that when it came time for Radha to choose how she and her soulmate would be united, that lack of self-love was behind each choice she made. She thought, "Lord Krishna deserves a young virginal mate, not one who is nine years older than he is and one who has borne three sons. So instead of verbalizing: "I want you to love and cherish me. I want you to shower me with flowers and gifts. I want you to be my loving husband." Radha chose for Lord Krishna to marry a young and virginal bride (Rukmini) who would be his physical mate. She chose for Radha-Krishna to be united through astral projection and never to physically lie with him. As if all that were not sufficient, Radha chose for Lord Krishna to break her heart and never speak to her until she had become enlightened herself. Radha had set herself up to fail with her horrible choices because she would only be able to reach enlightenment if she were able to forgive Sri Krishna for breaking her heart. She did however allow herself one grace which was that once they both had ascended into the light; she would become his life-long companion. But alas, things do not always work out as we had planned them.

II
Radha's Origin

Radha was born to a humble family who were immigrants to the U.S. of Middle Eastern origin. Her father was an intelligent and self-made businessman with the spirit of an entrepreneur. He had migrated to the U.S. by ship, deported at Ellis Island with all the other immigrants searching for a new life in "The Land of Opportunity." He performed manual labor picking beets on farms then progressed to working at one of the automotive companies. He had become a shop owner, the owner and manager of multiple rental properties, and much of the money he made, he had sent back to his homeland to educate his two brothers. He loved his daughter Radha and admired her intelligence. His dream was for her to complete her higher education (something he had never been able to do) and become a doctor one day. He often told his friends, "I want her to grow up to be a doctor."

Radha had chosen to be born a middle child with an elder sister of delicate health and a younger brother. That middle child syndrome and what she perceived as the lack of fairness or equality was one of the lessons she had come to learn about. The first-born sister needed additional care and attention as she had been born a premature twin while the other twin had died at birth. This caused Radha's mother to take extra care of her delicate first born. When Radha's mother learned that she was pregnant for a second time, her first extinct was to terminate the pregnancy. She even wrote to her family back in the Middle East requesting a prescription drug used there to cause the pregnancy to be terminated. The drug failed because the unborn Radha had planned it that way. But instead of coming into the arms of a loving mother who awaited her birth, Radha was born to one who dreaded her birth. She had heard her mother tell them stories of how when she was an infant, her mother would give Radha a bottle of milk as her feeding, only to come and find that her older sister had stolen the bottle out of her grasp and was suckling on it herself while hiding behind the sofa. Her mother always smiled when reminiscing about these incidents, and Radha wondered if she had ever worried that her second born was not being nourished properly. In her early years, when Radha and her older sister often would be running while playing together, blood would gush unstoppably from her sister's nose. Radha vividly remembers how her inept mother would lift the child over the kitchen sink as she bled profusely. Her father would be called home from work, and her sister would be hurried to the Emergency Room. Radha was blamed and spanked each time for making her older sister run. Even as a child she would think, "That is not fair. She should know better since she's older." So, Radha's struggles began while she was still in the womb fighting for her life as an unwanted fetus.

Radha only learned about her mother attempting to terminate her pregnancy many years later. She was in the kitchen and overheard a private conversation that her mother was having with another female friend in the adjoining family room. Her mother was recounting the sorrow of losing a child she had carried in her womb for seven months and the hardship of caring for a delicate premature newborn who after a lengthy stay in the incubator was still so small and delicate that they had been forced to carry her around on a pillow to prevent breaking her bird-like bones. Her mother admitted to taking the drug her family had sent her, but to no avail. When Radha heard this, it broke her heart as it would for any six-year-old child to hear that he or she had been unloved and unwanted. She marched into the living room shaking with rage, stood before her disconcerted mother who had no idea what she had overheard, and then raised her palm and proceeded to slap her mother across the face. People probably read this and react in different ways: Some may say what an insolent child Radha was. Others who have suffered the same fate may condone the behavior and empathize with Radha. What the reader must understand is that slap was not the reaction of a child, but the reaction of the God consciousness within the body of a child. Remember that each time you talk to or interact with a child. The body is that of a child, but there may be an old soul buried within.

Radha's numerology destiny number was three. Threes are born to learn about Equality and Communication. Those lessons that Radha had chosen were preparing her for the final leg of her evolutionary journey. She was born in 1963 in one of the eastern states of the United States.

1963 was a year of racial strife. Martin Luther King Jr. lead the March of twenty thousand people on Washington, on August 28, 1963 which was considered by MLK to be one of the "Greatest demonstrations of freedom at that time." This was the day he delivered his famous, "I Have A Dream" speech. She was born in a neighborhood demographic that was predominantly African American. Most of the neighborhood children she played with were children of color. Radha remembered calling one of her friends on the phone one day and asking to speak to her. She heard the voice at the other end state, "Oo you got a lit'l white girl for a friend." To Radha, this was her friend. She made no differentiation between color, but it seems the adults around her did. She felt as if she had done something unacceptable, when in actuality, the adults were teaching their children to see differences instead of unity.

Radha's father, although a minimally educated immigrant, was a man who believed in equality and freedom. When he came home each evening, Radha would sit on his lap as he recounted how he had hired African American workers to chop down evergreen trees from his farms to sell as Christmas trees in December. Once the trees had been loaded and delivered, he would take the workers to a restaurant to give them a meal. The waitress would say, "I'm sorry sir! We can serve you, but we can't serve them." Her father would reply, "Ok. Give me the chicken dinner, two steak dinners, etc." Once the food had arrived, he would give each gentleman a choice of a dish and keep one for himself. He was a man respected by his employees and admired by his peers.

III
Radha's Early Life

Radha lost her father to cancer in 1971. She was only eight years old at the time and since her father had been the buffer against the lack of love she felt from her mother and the adoration given to her younger brother who was to carry on the family name, she felt his loss the greatest. He was the one who had understood her best. Following the demise of her father, her mother removed Radha and her older sister from the public school they had attended and enrolled them in a private Catholic school called St. Mary's. Radha's family was not Catholic. They were not even Christian. They belonged to a religious sect that was considered a Muslim sect since they believed in one Almighty God or Allah, but in every other sense it was different. Their sect believed in reincarnation and in the suffering of the soul on its journey to salvation.

On condition of their enrollment, St. Mary's School required that they attend morning mass even if they were not Catholic. Radha's mother agreed and she would drop them off in the morning before school. Radha's fourth grade teacher unlike her older sister's teacher was not a nun. She had privately whispered to her that she could remain seated at the end of the service eliminating the need to take communion like her classmates since she was not Catholic. But to Radha, it made no difference. It was only bread and a little red wine. Just because they said it was the flesh and blood of Christ did not make it so.

Radha grew up with a love for Mathematics and Science. Algebra and Biology were her favorite subjects, and she was an 'Honor Roll Student' throughout her middle and high school years. Her father's dream may have been accurate, and she would become a doctor. But Alas, the universe and Radha herself had made a different plan.

Radha was not like other teenage girls. She had no wish to experiment with cigarettes, alcohol, marijuana, or even pre-marital sex. It was as if deep down she knew she was destined for something bigger. She fit in well and was not ill adapted in middle and high school, but she did so by having a group of loyal female friends who she hung around with and who did not pressure her into doing anything that made her uncomfortable. She even attended her ninth-grade prom with a group of those young women. She would hear her peers talk about their baby-sitting escapades and describe how they had put the three-year-old child to bed and then walked with the six-month old baby in the stroller down to the corner to smoke marijuana joints with friends. She was utterly astounded how they could expose a young infant to such danger. That was totally unfair to the infant, and she would emphatically state that. Her classmates would reply, "What do you expect, that we should put the baby to sleep and take the three-year-old, so she can tattle to her parents about us?"

Her high-school education was interrupted when her mother decided due to pressure from her Middle Eastern relatives that it was not proper to raise two teenage girls in the American culture. Her mother's relatives were afraid that Radha and her older sister would be tempted into following their peers down a wrongful path. They did not know that regardless of where a child is brought up, they will be following their own internal and chosen path. So, her widowed mother took them back to her country of origin and enrolled them in school there. All these events were written in Radha's destiny. Each time she paid for a jyotisha (astronomical reading of her destiny) to be performed for her, the pandits always informed her that her life would be filled with many unfinished and interrupted goals. That was so true of many of her life events. Her schooling appeared chopped up from being moved around from school to school during her elementary days or from country to country during her high school years. She was admitted into an American university in her mother's homeland, began to major in Biology, then civil strife broke out in the region, the president of the university was assassinated, the airport was closed, and Radha and her older sister were forced to flee the country by ship. This all occurred as Radha completed her junior year at university. Another disruption to her education.

She returned to the U.S., her country of birth, and attempted to transfer her credits and continue her university degree, but she became frustrated when she was informed that due to the American University losing its accreditation during the war, she would only be able to transfer thirty of her ninety completed credits. That was a loss of money and precious time that she had not anticipated. She decided to switch majors since more of her English credits had transferred than her Biology ones. She enrolled as an English major with a minor in Psychology

IV
Radha's Marriage

During her studies in the U.S., a young man whom she had met while residing abroad and grown attached to asked for her hand in marriage. Her mother was set against it especially since this marriage would require Radha to reside abroad in the Gulf region where he was employed as a civil engineer. He was employed by a renowned company that constructed palaces for the Royal family. Her mother's objection was not that he would not be able to provide for her, but that she would be leaving her university degree incomplete and living in a country so far away from home.

One day as Radha and her fiancé strolled around her U.S. neighborhood discussing what their future life would be like, he asked her a question: "Do you love me now more than you ever could?" Radha contemplated the question and then answered truthfully. "I think I will love you more after we have been wed and have had children." His response was not what she had expected at all. He became angry instead of happy. Enraged, he curled his fingers into fists and punched a nearby tree as if he wanted to do the same thing to her." A shiver of fear ran down Radha's spine. Suddenly a whisper coming from within warned her saying, "This man is going to hurt you for many years to come." That premonition or moment of intuition frightened her. It even gave her second thoughts about proceeding with the wedding plans, but she also understood that the only way her consciousness could have known what would transpire in the future was if she had created and chosen that for herself.

She was married in September 1984 via civil service followed by a large reception for family friends. A premonition of what lay in store for her future occurred on their wedding day. Radha had been told to prepare a large gift wrapped and slotted box for guests to drop their cards containing money. When a bride is travelling abroad, it is customary to gift them money or gift cards instead of items they cannot transport. She spent time wrapping the box in lovely wedding embellished wrapping paper and even included a large white silk bow. But when her groom saw it, he declared, "You are not taking that with you! It looks like we are asking for handouts." Radha complied, but later regretted it when people left their cards lying on tables and she was warned that one of the waiters or waitresses might take one or more of them. She did not depart for the country that would be her new home until a few months after that. Hence, began the first of 21 years of emotional and physical suffering. Her husband was very controlling, abusive both emotionally and physically. But Radha was not a passive victim. She gave back what she got. She would hit back, call him names, and rebelled against his dictatorial nature. His upbringing was totally different from the beliefs she had learned about freedom and equality in America. He wanted to control the trivial things in her life like what toothpaste or shampoo she used. Radha was an intelligent and educated woman. She did not feel it was necessary for any man to control every action of hers.

One weekend evening, a friend of theirs called her husband on the phone and invited them to come over for an evening spent on their rooftop garden. In the hot and humid Gulf region, it is not often that you have a cool evening to relax outdoors. Radha ran to the kitchen and immediately began to wrap up a tray of chocolate cupcakes that she had made the day before for her own sons. She knew that their friends also had three children who loved her cupcakes. She wrapped the transparent plastic tray in clear plastic wrap and added a bow. She then proceeded to go to the bedroom to change for the evening. When she finished dressing, she returned to find her husband standing with the cupcake tray in hand looking displeased. "What's this he asked?" "I'm taking those for their children, Radha responded. They like my cupcakes," she added. "No!" he stated. "You are not taking these. There are only ten of them and if she wants to treat our boys along with her children, there will be nothing left. It is shameful to take only that many," he stated as he tossed the tray on the dining room table. Radha tried to explain that if they had been invited to dinner, she would have baked them a large tray of twenty or more cupcakes, but this was an unplanned visit for them to drink tea on their rooftop garden. He would not listen. She reasoned with him and still he would not consent. In the end Radha said, "Fine. I have no wish to go. You can take the children with you and explain to them why your wife did not join you." Then and only then did he relent and permit her to take the cupcakes.

People may laugh that such a stupid argument could

have ensued over something so trivial as cupcakes, but that is exactly how toxic relationships thrive. The Ego turns small and insignificant things into major life changing events that at times even become violent and life-threatening.

Often Radha would rebel and put her foot down when she felt he was being unreasonable. Then the sun would set, and it was time for so called marital bliss, Radha would in her anger refuse him. That is when he would declare that she was his possession, and he was free to do with her as he pleased. He would shout with flaring nostrils and a pointed index finger that she had no right to refuse him his conjugal rights. That voice of intuition inside her spoke again and stated. "He can only possess your body, not your soul!" Those words gave her comfort and strength and made her understand that even though her life appeared to be a prison within the confines of a marriage to a despot, her soul was free.

Her marriage was a volatile relationship that they had chosen to be in together. Each of their souls had selected the other to teach it necessary lessons and to create suffering for it. Their marriage had provided Radha with powerful and controlling in-laws who also expected to dictate what she wore, whom she associated with, and even how she raised her three sons. Radha brought up her children to believe in Santa Claus, the Tooth Fairy, etc. as she had been brought up during her early life in America. An incident occurred when her oldest son lost one of his baby teeth. Radha told him that they would wrap the tooth in a tissue and place it under his pillow that night. The Tooth Fairy would come, take the tooth, and leave him a coin as a reward. One of her sisters-in-law immediately jumped up and declared that Radha was raising the boy to be a fool who would be laughed at by his friends because he believed in such fanciful characters. Radha tried to convince her that all these beliefs did was bring a little joy into a child's life. It would in no way contribute to the child's intelligence or acceptance in society. Her sister-in-law would not hear of it. She marched the little boy to her, spun him to face her and in no uncertain terms told him there was no such thing as a Tooth Fairy and that his mother was lying to him. The young boy's lip trembled as he attempted to hold back tears. Radha was shocked. In the American culture no one was permitted to interfere with a parent's upbringing of their child. Her sister-in-law had just crossed the line and infringed on Radha's freedom. Radha remembered this incident many years later when that same sister-in-law who had been at that time unmarried, had married, had two daughters of her own and those daughters believed in Santa Claus.

Radha was a science and English teacher while she resided in the Gulf. She had been teaching for many years and had been saving her salary for the time when she would break free from her unhappy marriage. It was the year 2006 and for many months Radha's intuition had been telling her that it was time to move on. She had learned the lessons she was meant to throughout the marriage and it was time for it to end. Radha knew that her husband would never agree to her leaving him and taking their children with her. She decided her only course of action would be to inform her principal that this school year would be her last. She explained that she was moving back home to the United States so that her older sons could attend university. Whenever any of her colleagues or the principal saw her husband at Parent-Teacher conferences, they always asked how he would fare on his own after Radha and the children were gone. Her plan had worked. She had forced her husband's hand and there was no way he could say that she had lied. That year, Radha began to donate unwanted clothing and items she no longer needed. She was preparing for a clean break. She purchased airline tickets for herself and her three sons. The oldest was twenty and had already completed his first year of college while residing with his aunt in the U.S. The youngest was only eleven at that time. In 2006, the internet was being widely used at schools and in homes. Radha was able to locate an apartment for herself and her children via a virtual tour of multiple apartment building complexes. She selected one in her home state that was near to where her mother and sister still resided. She also wired them the money to pay for the down payment. At the end of July 2006, she was back home in the U.S. awaiting a new chapter and a new beginning to her life.

V
Radha-Krishna

The first item on Radha's agenda was to find employment and to continue her interrupted university degree as an educator of Biology and English. In the U.S. she would need an updated teaching certificate prior to returning to her profession of teaching. She lived in an area surrounded by many universities and colleges. She now just needed to find the one best suited to her needs. She gained employment as a substitute teacher during the day, so that her afternoons and evenings were free to complete her studies. Some of the universities she visited did not offer evening courses in her selected major. Others would not allow her to begin without having all her past transcripts on hand. There was one university that did offer the courses she needed in the evening and it allowed her to begin study that January 2007 with a three-month grace period to have her transcripts sent in. That university just so happened to be in a city where a river (Yamuna) flowed nearby.

It was as if the universe had closed off all avenues and was guiding her towards this one specific university. Their Mathematics Department required her to sit for a Mathematics Placement test and were amazed at how well she had performed after being out of school for so many years. The director of the Mathematics Department informed her that she had placed in Math 110. There is a course being offered now, but it is full. Email the professor and ask if he will permit you as an extra. Radha emailed the professor and received a terse one-line response stating, "I do not accept extras." Radha added her name to the waiting list and hoped for the best. Each day she checked the roster and found her name was still on the waiting list. Radha had almost given up hope, because it was not until the very day the class was to begin when another student had dropped the course that Radha's name was moved onto the roster. She was in!

She sat along the side wall of the large classroom. She had checked the Professor's ratings online and had read that he explained well, but some students had stated that he spoke with an accent and was at times hard to understand. At the exact moment the class was to begin the professor arrived. He was young, younger than her forty-four years it seemed. He first began by stating that he would read off the names on the printed roster he held. Radha hoped he had printed off the roster that morning or else her name would not be on it. He read off the names, mispronouncing some as he read, then he got to her name. He pronounced her name Maya (the illusion). That is not how her family and friends pronounced her name, but she nodded when he asked if that was correct.

The days continued and each Math session Radha noticed how polite and respectful this professor was. Each day he would thank the students for coming to class and for giving him their time. One day when a professor in a nearby classroom was lecturing loudly, he suddenly went quiet with his ear cocked. They waited expectantly for what he would say and when he did speak, he joked, "The university should charge you double because it seems you are taking two classes at once." All the students laughed and smiled. Another day as he was lecturing, he stopped, and his eyes moved to the open doorway behind them. Radha turned to see what had caught his attention and there was an attractive young woman, most likely a former student, who was passing in the hall and had stopped to give him a little wave and a smile. The thought immediately came to Radha that she would never have the courage or confidence to do that herself. Why would such an odd thought come to her?

Radha had befriended a mature married woman in the class. They would sit in the front row to see the board properly and to take notes. The professor was in his early thirties, single, and kind. Radha's married friend noticed that he would come to class wearing a wrinkled shirt and she stated, "I have a friend that I would like to hook him up with." Radha's inner intuitive voice whispered, he is celibate and does not want to be hooked up. How odd! It was as if her soul knew him even though her physical avatar did not. One spring day, the sun shone bright and warm after the wet and rainy season had passed. Radha decided it was time to switch from trousers and closed shoes to a skirt and open sandals. Her toes were painted red and her feet looked tanned. She was sitting taking notes and suddenly felt this tingling in her feet. She looked up and found the young professor admiring her feet in the oddest way. She wondered if he had a "foot fetish". Flames of fire seemed to be moving along her bare feet and up her crossed lovely legs. His eyes seemed to be carrying on a slow seduction as they moved from the tips of her toes to her calves. Radha had never experienced anything so sensual in her life and her cheeks flushed as she slid her bare feet under the chair. Radha knew she had curvaceous and shapely legs that she had inherited from her mother. She had often received compliments from her female friends who wished they had legs like hers.

The professor had scheduled their first test in the course and although Radha had been studying at home and solving Math equations, there was one equation that continued to give her problems. She decided to go see the professor during his designated office hours to ask for help. She waited outside the office door until another student was done and then entered the office when he ushered her in. There was a long sofa along one wall, a chair opposite, a desk with ginger tea packets on it and shelves filled with origami swans and other animals. Radha sat on the sofa and waited for him to finish work on some papers. He then smiled and asked, "How can I help?" Radha showed him the equation in her notebook and explained that she continued to get a different answer than the one provided in the back of the textbook. He looked at her work, said the first part was correct and then stated, "Here is the problem. You must foil here. Didn't they teach you how to foil in India?" Radha was shocked. She did have dark hair and dark eyes, but that was the first time anyone had ever mistaken her for Indian. "I'm not Indian she stated." He began to question her about her origin even though she was reluctant to give out too much information. She finally told him where her parents originated from in the Middle East. "Oh! He said, "You have good food and good bread. The bread here in the U.S. is terrible. What kind of country doesn't know how to make bread?" He declared emphatically. Radha smiled and agreed. She then asked him if his home country had good food. He shook his head as if he was not a fan of his culture's cuisine. Radha was wearing a long handkerchief skirt with a top that had a long linear carmen neckline that extended towards the shoulders. As they talked, the edge of Radha's collar had slipped down exposing her bare right shoulder. Again, she felt that tingling fire as his eyes rested on the creamy skin of her shoulder and her exposed bra strap, and once again in her modesty she pulled the collar up to cover herself.

It was the week following the proposed test while he was returning their papers when something profound happened. He handed Radha her exam paper and she looked at her A- grade to examine the errors she had made. Suddenly her arm that held the paper began to vibrate. At first, she thought it was one of the students at a neighboring desk drumming their leg up and down, or maybe even a slight earthquake. She looked up, but she appeared to be the only one feeling anything. The vibrating continued and became stronger until her whole astral body was vibrating like a tuning fork within her. What was this? She had never experienced anything like this. Suddenly her consciousness said, "You are feeling someone's soul." Radha began to look at each of the students in the class. Some were young and pimply. Others were distinguished older gentlemen returning to complete degrees. She looked at each one slowly turning her head to examine each as the professor continued to distribute papers. Each time her eyes set on one of the students in the class, that little voice of intuition would say, "No, No, No!" It wasn't until her eyes came to rest on the professor at the front of the class that her consciousness whispered, "Yes. That's the one."

Radha had become a TM meditator many years prior in 1994. She had progressed to the 'Advanced Siddha' status and had felt many deep experiences during her meditations. During that summer of 2006 before enrolling at the university, she had begun reading a book titled, The Disappearance of the Universe by Gary Renard. The book had been a steppingstone in the evolution of her consciousness. The book stated that this world was an illusion created by our Egos to keep us trapped here and prevent our spiritual evolution. Her meditations had become deeper over the years and she had begun to experience out of body experiences as if her astral body were floating away as she meditated. Radha remembered talking to the Head of the TM Center, Mr. Salim, after reading that book and although he had never read the book himself, he understood by its title what it was about. Radha explained that previously when she had used the mantra, they had assigned her, she felt as if she was diving into a swimming pool from above. She had used the analogy to clarify. She explained that now she no longer felt that anymore. The teacher smiled and nodded. He said, "you are no longer feeling the dive because you have become immersed in the unified field of consciousness." Radha teared up in joy. Her life's goal had been to attain enlightenment and to end her suffering. The teacher also began to explain about the role of Prakriti and Purusha. He said that 'Prakriti' is the feminine creative energy. She is the temptress. 'Purusha', on the other hand is the soul, the Self, or pure consciousness. The word literally means "man". It is said that through the union of Prakriti and Purusha enlightenment is attained. This is the twin flame experience that so many women long for. It was as if Radha was ready for this knowledge, because even though she had not asked, the knowledge was bestowed upon her.

In 2007, when Radha began feeling her professor's soul, she had been on a long spiritual journey that had finally led her to him. She continued feeling the vibration of her professor's soul as she sat in class not concentrating on what he was teaching any longer. It was the strangest feeling because she could even feel his soul as she drove home across the border into a neighboring city where she resided. How is this possible she wondered? She decided that if this was truly a soul mate experience she was having, then she needed to find out if the professor was deeply immersed in spirituality as she was. She planned another visit to his office under the pretense of another question. This time she purposely mentioned that she was a TM meditator. He asked her, "So you have heard of Krishna?" She nodded. She asked him if he meditated as well. He shook his head and said, "I do projections!" He was referring to the projections of the astral body. They talked more about spirituality and she told him that she had visited Maharishi's Vedic City in Iowa and that Maharishi Mahesh Yogi, the Founder of the TM movement, had a University there. He asked, "Do they teach Math and Science?" She nodded and told him that Maharishi even had published a book titled The Science of Being and the Art of Living. He told her about his friends and acquaintances who had gone to ashrams where they made them clean and mop the floors and to cook, etc. Radha could hear the disgust in his voice when he said they take their money and then make them work. "How will they attain enlightenment by cleaning and cooking?" Radha recounted the wonderful meditative weekends her TM teachers had planned for them where the teachers sacrificed their own time away from doing their meditation programs to cook and clean for them. The students would be busy performing asanas and pranayama as they were led by a dedicated student. He was impressed by that. It was during this visit when an older professor from a neighboring office who was unfamiliar to Radha popped his head through the open door and said, "Hey! Did you hear what happened to so and so?" My professor shook his head in refusal. The other professor then went on to recount how another colleague of theirs had just purchased a new Hummer which was parked in his garage. On Father's Day, the colleague's young son had informed his father that he was preparing a surprise and not to come into the garage. When the colleague was eventually beckoned to the garage, he found that his young son had spray painted the shiny new vehicle with the words HAPPY FATHER'S DAY DAD. I LOVE YOU! The other professor laughingly described how angry their colleague had become at seeing his new car destroyed. My sweet professor listened to the story quietly and then said, "He should not have become angry. The child acted out of love." Radha's heart melted at hearing those words. An ordinary man would have asked if the colleague's automotive insurance would cover the destruction, but this highly conscious professor thought only that the child's intention had been to express his love for his father. Radha was happy, blissful even. She felt as if she was walking on Cloud Nine. This man had a PhD in Philosophy and he was highly conscious. He could certainly be her soul mate

One evening Radha was working in the computer lab which was on another floor of the Arts & Sciences Building. She had gone to the rest room and was returning to her computer where she had left her belongings. As she walked in the hall, she noticed her sweet professor walking in front of her. He must have just left one of his evening classes. The Math Department had a policy whereby they gave the single professors the graveyard shift while the married professors got to go home early to spend time with their families. Radha admired his lean hips and the spring in his step as he walked. He must have felt her gaze or known that she was there, for he did a quick pirouette on his heel so that he was facing her and gave her a devilish smile with a twinkle in his eyes. She smiled back. He walked backwards continuing to hold her gaze until she had reached the door of the computer lab. He walked past the wall length glass window continuing to smile at her with a quirked brow. She felt special, cocooned in love. In the days that followed, Radha searched up the professor's name on the internet and found an image of him sitting crossed-legged, yogi style, beneath a very bare decorated branch that supposedly represented a Christmas tree. The tree looked decrepit with only a few decorations placed around it and for some reason Radha's heart went out to him. He looked so alone in that photo that Radha was overcome with love and the wish to make him happy at any cost.

The Math course came to an end on the day of the final exam. And of course, the sweet Math professor brought his flute to class to play for them to alleviate their anxiety. He was an accomplished flute player who played the flute, Pan flute, as well as the harmonica. He had chosen to play the tune "Yankee Doodle Came to Town." It was a kind gesture on his part and a beautiful experience, but somehow Radha felt unfulfilled as if her soul longed for some more meaningful tune. The Math course ended, but their friendship continued.

That summer of 2007, Radha's brother had wed, so she selected some of the traditional sweets from her Middle Eastern homeland to gift to her professor. He had a sweet tooth and she had more than once seen him demolishing a piece of chocolate cake that one of the office staff had shared with him. She gave them to him at the beginning of the fall 2007 semester. One evening in January 2008, she was leaving the building after an evening Biology lab. She found him standing with a young female Indian student. He was dressed in cream-colored trousers and a black buttoned-down shirt. He appeared so handsome! Radha said hello as she passed, and then stopped when he began to introduce the two women to each other. The young lady was flirting with him and stating that he looked Indian. They asked Radha's opinion and she looked at him adoringly but shook her head to refute that. "In India, they wear white to stay cool while he is wearing a black shirt" she stated. He agreed with Radha, and Radha felt happy that he had sided with her. The young Indian woman jokingly insisted that Radha should take another look. Radha had no qualms, as he was truly a sight for sore eyes. Her eyes savored every bulging muscle and the tightness of his trousers on his powerful thighs. Her eyes slowly moved from his leather closed shoes up the length of him and she realized he had become aroused by her appraisal. He immediately dissipated the tense moment by asking them to walk with him. As they walked, the young woman asked Radha if she was Indian. Radha replied that she was not, but that the professor had mistaken her for one on her first office visit. "You were wearing a sari." he stated. "No, I wasn't!" Radha said. "It was a long handkerchief skirt and a matching top". The conversation ended on a light note as the young woman informed him that she was going to have her father, the Indian Ambassador to the U.S., invite him to dinner.

Radha went home feeling elated at seeing him and thinking she had to meet him alone somewhere if she was going to tell him she thought he was her soul mate. The University had an open-door policy which meant that professors could not close their office doors while a student was inside. How was she going to stand in his office with the door open and people passing in the hall and tell him that she could feel his soul? The reader is probably wondering why Radha was experiencing all these strange experiences, but her Krishna was not. Maharishi Mahesh Yogi had a beautiful quote that explained this:

"The nervous system of a woman is by nature more refined and much more delicate. She is the first to sense the good, the pure, the beautiful, the divine. By nature, man is more gross. His position is to deal with the world, so he must be able to deal with stress. Woman is balance, a balance of all nature."

So, her dear Kahn was probably thinking this was sexual attraction and had no idea that his Radha had been in his life for months. Radha decided she should email him and ask if they could meet somewhere for a coffee because she needed to tell him something private and important. Radha was oblivious to the destiny she had created for herself. She imagined she would tell him the news; he would rejoice in the news and they would be physically united as other twin flame couples are. The soul does not recall the plan it made for itself prior to its birth. That email she sent was misunderstood and misconstrued by her sweet professor, or so she assumed. His emailed reply was a hurtful and lashing response that broke her heart and whose words became engraved on her heart for the next twelve years.

VI
Radha's Broken Heart

The words to that email sent on that fateful January night in 2008 blurred as tears fell on her cheeks. The email said:

"I am not interested in you. I am not attracted to you. I don't ever want to see you again. Don't ever come to my office again. I am getting married this summer, so stay away from me."

Each of those statements drove a spear through Radha's heart. She threw herself on her bed and cried. She cried for hours as racking sobs shook her body. A popular song on the radio at that time was called "Bleeding Love" by Leona Louis, and the lyrics of the song seemed to describe Radha's pain perfectly. He had cut her open and instead of blood, she was bleeding love. All that pure divine love seeped out and was lost. Radha wondered how the universe could allow something so divine to be lost. The Ego which waits for opportunities such as this to hold us back began to whisper. "He forgot the plan. He thought that Indian girl was his Radha. He doesn't deserve for you to tell him." The damage had been done before their union had ever begun. Radha with her broken heart and wounded pride decided she would heed its advice and forget about telling him.

Life does not stop when our hearts are broken. Radha continued to attend her classes, write papers, perform labs. She did it all in an automated fashion, but in the moments when she was alone cooking in her kitchen, or taking a shower, or lying in her bed, the scalding tears would fall again. She kept her pain to herself because people could be so skeptical of anything, they had not experienced themselves. Even one of the TM teachers she had confided in said, "No! No soul mate would hurt you. This is not your soulmate." Of course, they did not expect that one of their students was the reincarnation of Radha, the Divine mother, herself.

Five months passed and Radha again was working in the computer lab printing off a large packet of lesson plans, exams, activity worksheets, and other documents that needed to be bound and submitted as a booklet for one of her Education courses. As she worked, she heard her Kahn's voice in the next room. He must have a class scheduled there. She had been working for hours and still required another hour or two. She picked up her cell phone and stepped outside into the hall to call her youngest son and let him know that she had cooked dinner and the food was on the stove top. As she stepped into the hall, she passed the door of the small lecture room that adjoined the computer lab. She glanced over her shoulder and found the professor's eyes on her. How had he known she was there? It reminded her of something Gary Renard had said in his book where he described seeing an aura around people and being able to see through walls as his vibrational frequency increased. She wondered if the same was true of her professor. She completed her phone call and returned to her computer. All the pain of the past months surged up again and enveloped her. She could not break down and cry in public. She needed to be strong and hold the tears in.

Her sweet professor's class had ended. She heard chairs scraping on the floor as they were pushed back, and students departed. Then she felt the power and energy of his gaze as his eyes bore into her bent head. She looked up and it was as if time stood still for a second. The atmosphere felt thick and tense as their gazes locked. He was walking past the glass windows of the computer lab as he had done the year before and he was staring at her. It was a hot and muggy day in May and Radha was wearing a short-sleeved T-shirt that clung to her firm breasts. Her dark hair was rolled up in a bun to keep it off her neck. Their eyes remained locked long enough for Radha to observe that there was a male student who was following him who appeared confused as to why the professor was going in this direction when his office was on the floor above in the opposite direction. Then Radha looked down before he could see the pain in her eyes or the tears that were about to fall. This time was so different than the last time they had met outside this computer lab when she had felt loved and cherished. The professor walked past the window and turned on his heel toward the swinging door that led to the stairwell. He was feeling some strong pent-up emotion as well, because with one abrupt thrust of his hand, he opened the door crashing it against the wall behind. What was he feeling Radha wondered? Was he feeling guilty at saying those horrible things to her? Was he regretting the loss of their friendship?

Another fall semester began, and if what her Kahn had said was true, then he had been married during the past summer. Radha searched the University Facebook page where they printed news of the faculty such as deaths, births, and even weddings. There was no news of his wedding. Had he just said those words to her to keep her away? It was early September, and that little voice of intuition would not be kept silent. It kept whispering to Radha, "You must tell him before it's too late." "You must tell him." Radha decided to make one more attempt to tell him but this time she would do it in person. She looked up his office hours and arrived at his office. The door was opened but the office was empty. Another professor in the neighboring office told her that he was in the photocopy room. Radha thanked him and said she would wait. She was terrified of his reaction. She was a soul with a broken heart now and had lost any confidence she once had. She stood and waited shaking on the inside. It takes courage to tell a man that you can feel his soul. What if he was a nonbeliever and laughed at her, or what if he became angry. She fled before he could hurt her again.

She went home after class and decided another email would be easier than seeing him face to face. But this time she would tell him directly and not ask to meet anywhere. She started the email by saying that she had gone to his office not to apologize, but to tell him that she loved him and had been feeling his soul ever since the Math course she had taken with him. She continued by stating that she thought he was her soulmate if he believed in such a thing. She ended by saying that her problem now was how to tell someone that you loved them when they had specifically told you that they were not interested in you, were not attracted to you, and never wanted to see you again. Tears poured down her cheeks as she typed the email and hit sent. She then waited for the outcome. She knew exactly when he had read it because she felt the vibration of his soul as it shook him to his very being. This was his Radha! Radha remembers feeling Krishna's pain a few days following. He was in utter agony and Radha ached to heal him. She didn't understand why he was in so much pain until many years later, but Krishna was aching for all the pain and suffering he knew his Radha would have to suffer.

Days went by with no reply. Would he really remain silent after she had told him such profound news? She decided another office visit was in order. She arrived just as he was leaving. He was locking the door to his office. She said, "Oh! You're leaving?" "I have a meeting," he said. "Can we talk?" Radha asked. He avoided meeting her eyes and said in his sweet voice, "We will talk another time." That sounded so ominous. The reader probably wonders at this strange behavior. Instead of taking his soul mate's hand and reassuring her or even replying to her email, he just went silent. Radha was confused too. It was only after their astral union began and her consciousness began to evolve that she realized what she had done. In that other dimension before being born on this Earth, Radha had decided that Lord Krishna deserved a mate that was young and virginal: She had told him to take a bride (Rukmini) that would make him happy and to use his astral projection techniques to unite them. Radha would still be his shakti or his Prakriti (the creative feminine energy) that he needed to evolve and become self-realized. She had made the ultimate and unconditional sacrifice of depriving herself of being with him physically as his mate to give him what she thought would be better for him. To love another more than oneself and to wish for his happiness even if that did not include her. That is unconditional love. The only problem is Radha had also told him to break her heart with the condition that he should never speak to her until she had become enlightened or self-realized herself. No words meant lack of communication especially when kind words were needed to heal her broken heart. She had closed off all avenues and all attempts for help.

The reader probably questions how it is possible for a soul to create so much suffering for itself. Well look at all the souls around you that die in car crashes or are murdered and raped. Those souls also created extreme suffering for themselves. For some, their suffering was quick as death followed; for others they may have suffered physically or emotionally for prolonged months or years. Radha's suffering lasted twelve long years.

VII
The Astral Union

In the days that followed Radha's visit to her Kahn's office, she began to feel this flutter and whooshing of energy that seemed to be coming ever closer to her. She did not understand what it was or what was happening. She grew sad and tearful. She thought aren't soul mates supposed to be joined when they meet? Shouldn't we be together instead of each of us alone and me crying myself to sleep?

There were so many confusing things happening to her. So many unexplained events. Then one day while she was at school subbing in a middle school classroom, her answer came. She felt that energy hovering around her again, but then it touched her. It was a soft and feather light kiss that landed right on her lips. Her lips tingled to such an extent that Radha lifted her finger and placed it on her lips. It was him. It was her Kahn. He was projecting to her and he was able to find her regardless of where she was, at home, at work, on campus. She smiled in joy that they were together in spirit even though they were miles apart.

The greater shock came the following day while she was at her physics class on campus. She was wearing a jean skirt and top. She was sitting with her notebook on her lap to take notes and a pencil case full of pens and rulers was resting on the extended arm used as a table. The professor was reviewing for the test they would be having in two days' time. As Radha sat there, she felt that familiar energy hovering near her, but this time instead of touching her lips, there was a powerful thrust straight between her legs and into her womanhood. Radha jumped, the notebook crashed to the floor, the pencil case and all its contents went flying. Several classmates were on their knees helping her to pick up her scattered belongings. Radha with head lowered and cheeks flushed thanked them and sat down. She was shocked at what had just happened. He was uniting them with his astral powers. Radha left class that day wondering what her doctor or anyone else would say if she told them that she was being made love to by astral projection? Would anyone believe her? Would they think she had lost her mind? And would a physical check up by her gynecologist reveal that she was sexually active?

This sexual onslaught continued daily from the moment she woke up until the sun set. It happened while she was at home, in class, while she drove to campus. It was relentless and Radha felt like she was a flower having its very essence sucked out of it. Some days she was happy and blissful knowing he was with her. Other days she cried and wondered why such a young, virile, and handsome man would want to unite with his soulmate in this way. She even questioned why this sexual union only occurred during the day and not at night. She did not know it then, but the nights were saved for his wife Rukmini. One night as she lay in bed alone, she reached out to him with her astral body and nuzzled his neck below his left ear. He responded with more sexual thrusts. He could sense her just as she could sense him. One day during her final exams, Radha was unable to concentrate. How can you study for a Chemistry final while you are sexually uniting with your lover? Radha spoke to Krishna and begged him to please stop. He responded by whispering that her studies were unimportant because they would become enlightened and he would take care of her. But deep down she felt the inkling that this union was going to go wrong, and she would need her teaching degree to support herself and her children. However, he was considerate enough to stop. Another time she was crying as they united. She cried because those hurtful words he had said to her had never been healed. Those words were engraved on her heart and she often felt she was being used instead of loved. If those hurtful words had been said to a soul that was confident and loved itself, the soul would have laughed them off and said, "Of course you love me. You are my soul mate." But not Radha. They had left deep scars in her heart and had provided the opportunity for her Ego to use those doubts. Their astral union continued until Radha felt Krishna's ascension. She knew he was no longer on the physical plane. She cried out to him, "Please don't leave me here." He promised that he would not. This is when he told her that she would be eternally blessed for her service to him.

Radha had read many online articles about Radha Krishna. She would read and shake her head at how wrong they were. Some would state that Rukmini had later become Krishna's shakti. That was not possible as Rukmini was introduced to spirituality in 2013 many years after Krishna had ascended into the light. Radha laughed at their ignorance and at the author's Egos that made them believe they know Radha-Krishna. Rukmini was Krishna's wife and a good wife at that, but never his shakti. Radha was Krishna's shakti and in the giving of her creative feminine energy, she lost her feminine creative energy and her ability to procreate. The people who think they know Radha write that she later went on to marry and have children. They have the story all wrong. What mere man could ever fulfill Radha after being with the perfect Krishna. How could she later bring forth offspring into the world when she had lost her ability to ovulate? Early menopause her gynecologist called it.

VIII
A Change in Destiny

Radha and Krishna's original plan had been that once they had both ascended into the light, Radha would continue as Krishna's life-long companion. He would be the mentor to her three sons and guide them in their spiritual evolution. That was of course if she could heal from the broken heart and ascend. They had chosen to reside in a small and humble home close to nature since worldly possessions would no longer have any meaning for them. That Radha would cook healthy vegetarian dishes for them. They would be spiritual mates on their evolutionary journey. However, her broken heart allowed Radha's Ego to change the plan. Her Ego stated, "What soulmate says those horrible words to his soulmate? What woman wants to spend the rest of her life with a man who has broken her heart?" Radha decided she no longer wanted to continue with the plan she had made. As her Kundalini rose like fire from her Root chakra to her Crown chakra, she began to see a golden light. At the end of the light was her Lord Krishna with hand outstretched waiting for her. Radha saw him there, felt fear that he would hurt her again, and turned away. It is common knowledge that Radha-Krishna had the ability to speak to each other.

She made the decision to discontinue the plan. She said, "I no longer wish to be your wife, your queen, or a God." I am happy you have another who loves you. I just want to live in peace for the rest of my life, and never be hurt again." He whispered, "But you chose this. If you turn away now, you will suffer for many years to come." It is true, Radha had seen herself standing before Krishna and asking for this astral union. She had chosen this, but she had never envisioned how painful those choices would be. She felt used and dumped as men have used women for centuries. She believed herself to have been betrayed and she lashed out at her Kahn, insulted him by calling him names that women call the men who betray them. She had reached the pinnacle of spiritual evolution. She had seen a gold chariot with herself and Krishna riding in it. She had felt egoless and experienced the peace and unconditional love that envelopes you as you become enlightened. But instead of welcoming that, she had rejected it all because her Kahn had broken her heart. Radha had made the ultimate sacrifice and instead of the expected gratitude, her heart had been broken leaving her with a painful soulmate experience that left her wanting to escape.

Radha's life changed after that as did Krishna's. Her perception of her Kahn came crashing down from that divine pedestal she had set him on. She perceived him as the man who had hurt his love. She continued with her higher education, received her teaching degree, and began teaching. Her professional circumstances had improved, but spiritually, she was a broken soul. Krishna had never worn a wedding band when he first married Rukmini. The wedding band is a symbol of possession and he was stating that he was not her possession but that of Radha's. However, after Radha had chosen not to be his life-long companion, he began to wear a wedding band stating that his body now belonged to Rukmini. He resided in a luxurious home with hard wood floors, granite kitchen countertops, and a yoga studio. Radha lived in a humble home close to nature. She owned a pet dog who loved her unconditionally and slept at her feet. She would never throw bread or food away, but instead would place it outside in the woods to feed the birds and squirrels. She was like "Snow White", a princess living a simple life in the woods. She worked hard as a teacher, was adored by her students, and was fulfilled in the changing of young lives. And through it all, that intuitive voice within would say, "You could be so much more." Radha had a small hanging plaque in her kitchen that read, "A person is only as big as the dreams they dare to live." Radha's fear of being hurt again by her Kahn had prevented her from daring to live. She lived a normal life of suffering for some years instead of the one she had been destined for.

Rukmini's life and destiny were changed along with the change in plan. She became Krishna's queen. He first enrolled her at a community college to get a degree. This was followed by a Yoga school in India, so that she could become a certified Yoga instructor and continue her spiritual evolution. Finally, he enrolled her in an Ayurvedic Course to learn about healthy cooking, eating, and the use of alternative treatments for ailments. Krishna was setting an example for all men by showing them what a good husband should do; he was an epitome of how a husband should support and guide the evolution of his wife, help her to complete her academic education, support her financially, and mentor her on her spiritual journey. Rukmini in Sanskrit means one who is adorned in gold. Rukmini was showered with all the jewels she desired. Every wish of hers was consented to by Krishna, because by giving Rukmini he was giving Radha and all the women of the universe. He was repaying Radha for the gift of her shakti. Rukmini travelled the world with him. He took her to France, Italy, Japan, Kuwait, and India, and through it all Radha followed their travels through social media. She saw the images that Rukmini posted of them cuddled together and regretted her own loss. But the reader must understand that Krishna's and Rukmini's relationship following Krishna's ascension was platonic love. Krishna had lost all his carnal desires and needs. Rukmini was a good wife in the sense that she cooked his meals, washed his clothes, and hosted his guests. No children were ever brought forth from that marriage!

IX

Radha Meets Avdhoot Shivanand Ji

Radha's best friend through all these experiences was a young woman of Indian descent who was a Sikh by birth. She was married and had two sons who became firm friends with Radha's own sons. Her Indian friend had been given the name Monica at birth by her father who admired a celebrity with that name. Monica became Radha's confidante. Radha kept no secrets from her and shared everything with her from her meeting with Krishna, to him breaking her heart, and even the astral union that had followed. Radha was able to talk to her because she knew the story of Radha-Krishna.

Monica began to take Radha with her to their Sikh temple. Radha would listen to the chanting of Waheguru, Waheguru (one God) and tears would fall down her cheeks at the beautiful and divine meaning behind these words. The Sikh followers were impressed that the heart of this foreign follower was melting and would ask her what she was feeling and experiencing. But following the chanting, they would use a projector and screen to display English translations of what they were chanting for the many English-speaking participants. Radha would read, but when she saw the words, "Save Every Sikh", at the end, she knew that this

Sikh temple was like every other religion in the world that believed itself to be the "Chosen Religion." Any philosophy that doesn't preach true unity of all consciousness is lacking. She shared her thoughts with her friend Monica and with others in the temple. Some of the arrogant and egotistical men even looked down at her and scorned her as if saying who are you and what do you know. They had no idea they were in the presence of Radha. They tried to convince her otherwise, but Radha knew better. In her life, she had been exposed to Christianity in her childhood, Islam while she resided in the Gulf region and taught at Muslim schools, Krishna-Consciousness through her meditations and her TM movement. This Sikh temple was not for her.

Monica listened to and believed Radha about the unified field of consciousness. She stopped attending her Sikh temple when they sent her invites. Instead, she found a Guru online by the name of Avdhoot Shivanand Ji. She was so impressed with what he was saying that she phoned Radha one day and asked her to come over and watch him. Radha came, not knowing what to expect. Monica opened her laptop and played a video of Avdhoot Shivanand Ji speaking in Hindi. Radha could not understand the language. His voice was powerful and strong and resonated in the room. Monica was translating what he was saying into English for Radha's benefit. However, Radha did not need the translation. Her astral body began to vibrate at the voice of this enlightened Saint. Her Solar Plexus or Manipurak Chakra began to spin in a whirring motion like the spinning of a windmill. Radha immediately decided she needed to see this Guru.

A few days later Monica read that Babaji would be holding his first gathering in Toronto, Canada. Radha and

Monica decided that it would be close enough for them to drive from the U.S. They reserved their spots at the gathering and Radha paid for both her own and Monica's portion of the tickets which included a hotel reservation for the days they would be there. That is the way Radha was. She put the interests of others before her own and was aware that her friend did not have a full-time job or the funds to cover the trip.

When the awaited day arrived, they packed their bags in the back of Monica's SUV, filled the car up with gasoline for the long journey ahead, and brought along some munchies and snacks. They had also packed some extra tea and biscuits for the evenings in the hotel as well. It was a time for them to bond and talk as they drove across state lines. They arrived at their hotel the night prior to the beginning of the Shivir. The Shvir was being held in Swaminarayan Temple in Toronto Canada that March of 2012. The following morning, they arrived at the Shivir early to ensure they could complete their registration and receive their identification badges.

Monica saw some of her Shikh followers who it seems had also decided that maybe Shikhism was not the path to enlightenment. Each time Monica introduced Radha to someone, she would tell them this is my "sissy" (sister) and she would say she paid for my ticket and brought me. It was very sweet of her to wish to give Radha credit, but from Radha's perspective, she would not have come alone since the majority of the Shivir would undoubtedly be done in Hindi or another Indian dialect.

They entered the large hall and there were assigned seats depending on the amount participants had paid. The highest priced seats were located at the front of the hall near the stage where the two saints Babaji and his wife Guruma would sit. Radha's and Monica's seats were located in the middle. They could see the stage perfectly and as microphones were set up, they would also be able to hear everything. The stage was adorned with flowers and there was an alter set up for the Puja that would be performed at the beginning.

Babaji and GuruMa entered the hall from a secluded entrance near the back of the stage. They were accompanied by Sadiks whose job it was to set the microphones up and to adjust the red blankets that would be laid on their laps. Babaji looked out at the hundreds of people seated in the hall. He was using his Third Eye to see, because his eyes rested on Radha in the hall. Radha shivered as she realized he was looking at her aura. He then turned to GuruMa and asked, "What happened?" GuruMa whispered something back. That female perception again came into play. She realized that Radha was in the hall with them and she told him. Babaji nodded. He welcomed all the participants. "Welcome! Welcome!" he said. He then spoke to the gathered participants and stated. "Some of you are far more advanced than others" Of course, many assumed he was referring to them, but Radha knew he was referring to her. The Puja was performed and the Shivir began with an explanation of the positions of the seven chakras and breathing through pranayama which Radha was very familiar with.

Babaji in his exulted and enlightened state was able to address each consciousness in the hall without the others hearing. As he proceeded to do his cleansings and healings, he spoke to Radha. He stated, "He was not very loving? Was he?" The tears would fall uncontrollably from Radha's eyes and her consciousness replied, "He was horrible." Babaji then said, "It was your fault. You created this." Her TM teachers had stated the same, "You manifested this." It is true, she had created the astral union, the broken heart, and the lack of communication. She could blame only herself. Babaji cautioned Radha, "Don't hurt him he said. He is so loving right now."

It was at this 2012 Shivir when Radha had an unusual experience. In her TM and Sidha courses, the TM instructors had explained to them that as the consciousness evolves, it releases in different manners. Some people laugh, others cry, or as Radha was informed by her son when he completed his Sidha course that some men even release gas. These participants who were mainly of Indian descent looked down at Radha as Monica translated some of the questions that were being asked in Hindi. They questioned what this American woman was doing here? As Babaji's voice boomed loudly in the hall and he would yell "Release" as he commanded the Ego to let go, Radha began to whimper and cry softly. Her breathing was ragged as the agony and pain she had been living through was being released. All the participants were supposed to be seated with their eyes closed. Suddenly, Radha felt a cold wrinkled hand smelling of spices over her mouth. She opened her eyes and looked at the old Indian woman who was wearing a sari. The woman placed her index finger over her lips and said, "No sound. Hush!" Radha was stunned. This would never have happened at one of her TM centers. When the meditation was over, it was obvious that Babaji knew exactly what had happened to Radha. He was upset and disdainfully said, "I thought you were ready for this, but I was mistaken. You must respect others and the experiences they are having." Radha only shook her head at the irony of the situation. This was supposed to be a more advanced Shivir for those Sadiks who had already attended one prior. On that initial registration day, they almost denied Radha and her friend Monica entrance because they said neither had attended the first Shivir. If these were the more advanced group, then what are the beginners like? Radha wondered.

Radha and her friend Monica attended many of Babaji's Shivirs following that one. They attended one in Houston a few years later and another in Philadelphia. Monica even attended a few with some of her own family members while Radha was busy teaching during the school year. It was at one of those Shivirs while Babaji was performing what he called "The Art of Dying" that Radha was reminded of an incident in her early childhood. This meditation or sadhana was performed for the participants to regress back to past lives and to witness how they had died. It is a loud and frightening experience as many of the participants scream, yell, and at times begin to flail their arms. Radha's experience was not so dramatic. However, she regressed back to her mother's womb and saw herself trapped there. Her tiny fetal hands had been balled up into fists and she was pounding on the walls of her mother's uterus and crying to be let out. That is the moment when Radha remembered that fateful day in her childhood when her mother had said that she had attempted to abort Radha using pills. She was not only the recipient of the action but had become the witness as well. She had stood back and watched the event unfold as if she had not been the crying fetus.

X

Krishna Did Not Forget Radha

Many of the stories that Radha has read online state that Radha and Krishna never saw each other again after their separation. That is not true! Even after all the horrible words she had said to him, the way her astral body had shoved him away, and the astral lashing he had given back to her, he never forgot her. In 2010, Radha was hired as a long-term substitute teacher for a professor who had gone on sabbatical. She was now an employee at the same university where her Kahn instructed. She could feel him even when he was in another building nearby. One day as she drove from the campus to her home, Krishna was in the vehicle ahead of her. She recognized him from his rear-view mirror. He had stopped at a red light and as he turned his head, he looked at Radha, smiled, and jerked his head in motion as if to say, "Follow me." He was not referring to following his vehicle but to following his ascension into the light. Another famous song came to mind by Bruno Mars titled "Locked Out of Heaven". The lyrics of the song state, "You make me feel like I've been locked out of heaven." Those words summed up exactly how Radha was feeling.

In 2012, Radha was driving along a main freeway near

her home. She stopped at a red light again and smiled at a little girl waving at her in the SUV parked in front of her. Radha then looked over at the vehicle that was stopped beside her to her right, and there was her Kahn with Rukmini seated beside him in the passenger seat. Rukmini was chattering about something, but Krishna had eyes only for Radha. He smiled at her, but his smiles only brought Radha pain instead of pleasure. Her soulmate experience, in her perception, had been the worst thing that had ever happened to her. It was her perception that needed to change.

Life events are repeated in seven-year cycles, so the spring of 2014 was an important year for Radha since that was seven years since the year, she had fist felt the vibration of Krishna's soul. That spring, she received a request to connect on LinkedIn from her Mathematics professor. She checked out his LinkedIn profile, saw the glowing recommendation he had made for Rukmini as a certified Yoga teacher and was torn by jealousy. She kindly refused his request to connect with a sentence explaining that it was too painful for her. She heard him whisper, "Your heart still hasn't softened towards me."

In the fall of 2014, his astral body appeared to Radha multiple times. Once it was in her classroom at school while she was still setting up for the new school year. "You could be so much more." He stated. Radha only cried and said. "I'm happy and safe from being hurt here."

Once again, his astral body appeared to her in her bedroom a few evenings later. He stood silently near the door as if unwilling to intrude. She saw him and her consciousness said, "You hurt me so bad. I don't know if I will ever heal." Krishna softly but adamantly responded, "I'm not like that anymore."

XI
Radha's Suffering Ends

Those online articles that one reads state that Radha lead a hard and difficult life after Krishna. That is not completely true. The years between 2008 and 2014 were difficult for Radha. She was sad and cried often remembering the great love that she had lost. She would see his face in a large group and her heart would miss a beat as her eyes searched for him in a crowd. Radha's difficulties were also caused by her financial situation since her only source of income was the small annual salary, she made from her substitute teaching and the scholarship money she had received at university. That is when she decided to sell all the 22-karat yellow Indian gold she possessed from her marriage and from her years residing in the Gulf. The price of gold was up that year, so Radha took the many bangles, necklaces, and rings she possessed and sold them all. Some of those pieces she had purchased herself, others were gifts, and still others were part of her dowry. The shopkeeper was impressed with them and asked her where she had gotten all this high-quality gold since in the United States most of the gold is 14 karat and loses its yellow sheen after being worn. Radha was not vain and no longer was attached to these Earthly possessions. The story of how Krishna stripped Radha of all her jewelry while on the waters of the river Yamuna is also recounted.

However, between 2015 and 2020 her broken heart began to heal. She was able to reflect and dwell on the happy times she and Krishna had spent together. To reiterate, Radha was born under the number three destiny. That meant that she was physically strong and healthy. In her life, she had never suffered a broken bone or required a surgery of any kind. She was a creative person which was evident in the creative labs and ideas she devised while teaching her students. She was creative in the gifts she gave to family and friends. Her goal was to uplift and heal people and through her positivity she was able to set an example for others to follow. She often hummed and sang as she shopped and cooked. This was one of her trademarks. Instead of dwelling on the fact that she had lost Krishna, she rejoiced in the fact that she had been blessed to have loved and served him unconditionally. A famous quote by Lord Tennyson states, "Tis better to have loved and lost than never to have loved at all." Those words hold true because many people never have the advantage of knowing Sri Krishna, of being in his presence, of uniting spiritually with him, and finally being blessed by him.

The true goal of spiritual evolution is to know oneself. "Know Thyself" is a key phrase used in spiritual movements. Well Radha knew herself. She was the reincarnation of that famous Radha that lived so long ago. Although some of the events of her life may be slightly different than those of the past, but each time she is reincarnated as Radha, she will be older than Krishna, her heart will be broken by Krishna, she will love Krishna unconditionally and she will serve him by being his Shakti.

Radha was fully healed when she ultimately realized that she was not a victim. Her Krishna had not broken her heart. He had merely done exactly as she had asked because that is the quantity of suffering Radha felt would be needed to break the Ego of The Divine Mother. Radha's vibrational frequency began to rise again, because in 2020 she began to receive a plethora of Facebook friend requests from TM pandits in India. She would look to see what mutual friends they shared and see that her TM teachers were listed, so she would accept. Then they would send her a message saying, "I wish to be your friend." Radha would ask, "Why do you wish to be my friend?" The reply would be, "We are pandits. We read the forehead and heart. You love Krishna. You are Radha. We will worship you." Those words would bring tears of happiness to Radha's eyes. Her service to Lord Krishna had not been in vain, and in the spring of 2021 another seven-year cycle will have passed, and Radha's broken heart will have healed.

It was Radha's dharma to forgive Sri Krishna just as he forgave his followers. However, the irony is that there is truly nothing to forgive since he had merely done as she had requested in that other dimension. He had fulfilled his part in this play they were acting in. Her heart had been broken because her perception had been clouded and because those hurtful words, he had stated had brought up old wounds from her childhood. Krishna had united with her astral body, had never spoken to her again just as she had chosen. When she finally accepted that, no longer felt that she was a victim, and finally had the courage to merge with Krishna, she was at peace, shook her head at how critical of herself she had been to create such a soul-mate experience. She wanted to laugh and cry simultaneously. She was free from the web she had entangled herself in.

9 789354 387180